STAR MOTHER'S YOUNGEST CHILD

LOUISE MOERI

STAR MOTHER'S YOUNGEST CHILD

Illustrated by Trina Schart Hyman

HOUGHTON MIFFLIN COMPANY BOSTON

Library of Congress Cataloging in Publication Data

Moeri, Louise.
  Star mother's youngest child.

  SUMMARY: The grumpy old woman had never properly
celebrated Christmas until the year that the Star
Mother's youngest child came to earth to find out
what Christmas was all about.
  [1. Christmas stories] I. Hyman, Trina Schart.
II. Title.
PZ7.M7214St. [E]   75-9743
ISBN 0-395-21406-8

ISBN: 0-395-21406-8 REINFORCED EDITION
ISBN: 0-395-29929-2 SANDPIPER PAPERBOUND EDITION
PRINTED IN THE UNITED STATES OF AMERICA

BVG 20 19 18 17 16 15 14

To my mother and father, with love

There was once a woman who had outlived all her
own family of parents and sisters and brothers. Having no children or grandchildren of her own there
was no one to keep her company in her old age. She
had lived out her life in the hut her parents had left
her on the edge of the forest, and as the years passed,
the villagers — just over the hill — gradually forgot
she was there.

Once upon a Christmas the old woman sat drowsing and grumping before a low fire. Her tiny house was in order, the cow fed, the chickens shut up for the night, the water pumped, the wood brought in, and her solitary bowl of soup cooling on the table beside her. All was in order for the winter night, but still she rocked and grumped.

"Just once," she muttered, "only once. Is that too much to ask?" She darted a harsh glance upward, but all she saw were the ceiling beams, blackened by these many fires. "Just once, I'd like to have a *real* Christmas, with a Christmas tree, and presents, and candles lit, and music, and a feast —" She looked all around, but there was no one to talk to, no one to complain to, only her old dog sleeping and twitching on the hearth rug at her feet. "Uproar," she said to the dog, nudging him in the ribs, "you're a good dog, an excellent dog, but I can't celebrate Christmas with you."

Outside the wind blew as cold as the breath of frost against the little house and snowflakes lifted up from the drifts and ran about like little girls in white dresses. A wolf howled at the moon, and the shadows of the forest grew blacker and blacker as the night wore on.

At last the old woman tired of rocking and grumping. She ate her soup, and took off her clothes and put on her night dress and night cap, but just before she blew out the candle for the last time, she went to the door, opened it, and looked out. Seeing the vast canopy of stars overhead, all of them twinkling and shimmering up there together like some great family of acrobats in silver sequins, the old woman thrust back her head and shouted — right up at the stars — "Just once! I'd like to celebrate a Christmas! Is that too much to ask?"

And then she went to bed.

Now, there was another old woman who was troubled on that winter night. Up in the sky, the Star Mother was in great agitation. She was sweeping and smoothing the clouds, scrubbing the faces of the smaller stars, and cleaning the windows of Heaven so all of their brightest light could shine through. Worst of all, she was constantly bothered by the peevish whining of her youngest child. The Star Mother's Youngest Child — so new he had not yet been given a name — was dawdling and diddling around the sky, banging into constellations and scuffing up the clouds his mother had smoothed out so carefully. He fussed and he pestered, and nothing would please him.

Finally, in a rage, Star Mother seized a comet by the tail and waved it over her head. "Now, Youngest Child, unless you stop this chittering and chattering, this clittering and clattering, I'm going to thrash you!"

Youngest Child howled and hopped around, and sobbed.

"What's the matter?" cried Star Mother. "Here it is Christmas Eve, and of all nights of the year, the sky must be its most beautiful! And with all this work I have to do — cleaning and polishing and dusting and sweeping — I have to be bothered by a cranky Youngest Child!"

Youngest Child howled even louder. "Mother!" he wailed, "just once I want to celebrate Christmas like they do down *there!*" He leaned out the window and pointed to the earth, floating like an iridescent green Christmas bauble far below.

Star Mother put down her comet and stopped to listen, as all good mothers do, her hands on her hips and her hair all spangled with dust of stars. "Well," she said thoughtfully, "if that's all that's troubling you, I suppose it could be arranged — but only this once! Would it really make you happy, Youngest Child?"

"Oh, yes! mother," cried Youngest Child. "After all, by next year I'll have grown so big I'll have to take my place in one of the constellations, like all your other children, but this year — this Christmas — I would so love to celebrate with a Christmas tree, and candles, and presents, and music. Is that too much to ask?"

"Suppose not," grumbled Star Mother, smiling to herself. "Now, run along, and I'll think of a plan . . ."

Christmas morning dawned clear and cold. The forest behind the old woman's lonely hut was so still, so brilliant, in the first rays of the sun that one would have thought the whole world had been carved out of ice.

Sleepy smoke crept up from the chimneys of the village, and some time later the church bell began to chime. But even the sound of the bell did not rouse the old woman in the hut. She was deep under the coverlets in a deeper dream of — what was it? Music . . . ?

But then there was a sound that did wake her. Bang! Bang! Bang! "Hello, the house! Wake up! Wake up!"

Grumbling and wheezing, the Old Woman roused herself, threw back her blankets. Fumbling for her slippers, she drew a quilt around her shoulders and stumbled across the floor. "Who's there?"

The old woman opened the door.

There upon the doorstep stood the raggedest, ugliest, most unattractive child she had ever seen. He had patched up clothes of some uncertain style, a wrinkled brown face, and spiky, yellow hair that stood up like dry grass all over his head. Worst of all, he looked both cold and hungry.

"Well? Well?" shouted the Old Woman, who was a little deaf, and like all deaf people thought it was others who could not hear. "Who are you? What do you want?"

The Ugly Child stood blinking and shuffling on the doorstep. He seemed as nonplussed upon seeing the Old Woman as she was upon seeing him.

"Did you want to see me?"

"Not very bad," admitted the Ugly Child.

"Well?" shouted the Old Woman again. "What is it you want? We'll both freeze to death with the door open while you stand there tongue-tied."

"I was looking," said the Ugly Child at last, "for Christmas."

With a howl the Old Woman threw up her hands. "Mercy! Mercy!" she cried. "To be wakened on a freezing day like this by a vagabond whose wits have evidently frozen too! Looking for Christmas! I'll be bound — and where did you expect to find Christmas? *Here?*"

The Ugly Child peered past the Old Woman into the poor little hut. He carefully took in the shabby furniture, the bare table, the sparse stores of food and clothing. "Well," he muttered, "here is where I am."

The Old Woman was beside herself. With every passing moment the hut was getting colder, and her woodpile was none too large at best. "Oh, come in, come in!" she cried in exasperation. "At least it will be easier talking with you on the inside than on the outside!" She grabbed the boy's arm and dragged him unceremoniously into the room. Uproar, who was also deaf, awoke and dashed up barking but the Old Woman shushed him and sent him to sit under the table. He lay there blinking and scowling and licking his chops as he stared at the boy's skinny arms and legs; any one of them would have made him a welcome meal. What better use could there be of such an ugly child. . .?

"You're from the village, aren't you," said the Old Woman, peering at her visitor. "That's who you are — one of those rascally boys who come out here and steal my watermelons and chase my cow till she won't give down her milk? Out with it — what prank were you going to play on me today?"

The Ugly Child had walked over to look at the cold fireplace where only a few red coals glimmered in the ashes. "What's this?" he asked.

"Mercy!" cried the Old Woman, "anybody with half his wits can see that's a fireplace — and with the fire gone out, too. Here — help me lay the fire —"

She grabbed a handful of straw from a basket, and some twigs, and then a small stick or two. Kneeling on the hearth she fed first the smaller, then the larger fuel into the coals. With a great deal of snapping and popping, the fire woke up, began to eat the straw, and soon was blazing nicely. The Ugly Child, who was still standing idly by, stretched out a hand. "Pretty," he murmured.

"Ay, pretty it is," grumped the Old Woman, "but a kettle on to boil is even prettier. Fetch me the water pail in the corner." But the Ugly Child did not seem to know what a water pail was, nor even yet a corner. The Old Woman was forced to bring the water, fill the kettle, and start a bit of mush cooking. To settle her nerves and start her blood warming, she also made some tea.

The Ugly Child sniffed as the fragrance of steaming hot tea rose from her old pewter mug.

"Ugly brat," muttered the Old Woman. "Where did you get that huge nose — it's all wrinkled like a potato — or a rock — "

The Ugly Child blinked. He felt his nose. It was wrinkled. "Well," he said defensively, "you're not all that pretty, either."

The Old Woman stamped her foot, sloshing hot tea down her chin. "One more word like that and I'll send you packing!" she shouted. "I don't care who you are or where you come from — you'll mind your manners or be gone!"

The Ugly Child sniffed again. His brown face was a kind of dusty color and it almost seemed to change shape like a shifting tangle of rock and sand as he spoke. "What's that in the pot?" he asked. "Mush," said the Old Woman. "And I suppose you want some."

"I suppose so," said the Ugly Child, "if that's all there is."

The Old Woman was so angry she grabbed a ladle and slapped a great huge gob of hot mush into a bowl. Some of the mush splashed up on the face of the Ugly Child. The Old Woman stopped in horror — she had not really meant to hurt him — but instead of howling the Ugly Child reached out with his tongue and licked his cheek. "It's good," he said.

Somewhat taken aback, the Old Woman ladled out her own mush and put a jug of cream on the table. "Isn't any sugar," she said tartly, although it wasn't really true. She had some sugar hidden away but she certainly wasn't going to waste it on this little ragamuffin.

"What's sugar?" asked the Ugly Child.

When their bowls were empty, the Old Woman went into the lean-to and put on her workaday dress. She pulled on heavy woolen stockings and leather boots, and tied on a shawl and bonnet.

"What are you going to do?" asked the Ugly Child.

"Chores," snapped the Old Woman. "What else?" She took a couple of buckets from the bench and went out. The Ugly Child followed her.

The sun had risen into a dazzling blue sky but seemed not to have warmed the air at all. As they walked toward the cow shed their breath hung in front of them in a white mist and their noses pinched together.

The Ugly Child followed at the Old Woman's heels, while Uproar floundered beside them through the drifted snow. All the roofs were capped with heavy snow and the fir trees hung heavy with icicles that gleamed in the sun like festoons of diamonds.

"Hey!" cried the Ugly Child. "I see one! I see one!"

"What? What? Where?" cried the Old Woman, expecting a wolf at the very least.

"A Christmas tree!" cried the Ugly Child. He had left the path and gone a bit toward the woods, and he stood there pointing. His strange little face glowed and his spiky hair stood up as if the wind were blowing through it. Before him was a small green fir so plump and pretty it would have made a model for any Christmas tree in the world. Its feathery branches moved and the icicles danced and tinkled.

The Old Woman stared. Well, it *did* look a little like a Christmas tree . . .

"What do we do?" cried the Ugly Child. "Now that we've found our Christmas tree?" He was dancing around in the snow and yanking on the fringes of her shawl. "Is there something more we should do?"

"Well, I should think so," growled the Old Woman. "We have to cut it and take it inside the house. You certainly don't think a body can have a proper Christmas tree out here beside the cow-shed, do you?"

In a moment the Old Woman fetched her axe from the lean-to, cut the tree, and carried it into the house. "There, you dolt!" she cried in some irritation. "*That's* what a Christmas tree looks like!" She stuck the end of the trunk of the tree in an old leaky bucket and made it tight with rocks. And so it sat beside the fireplace, green and wonderful. "Well," said the Old Woman, pinching her lip between her fingers, "it lacks a few things yet . . ." And so she went about the house, opening boxes and drawers and fumbling on shelves and under the bed. At last she had assembled a little pile of things: bright yarn, an old thimble, a little bell, some broken beads. In a few moments her nimble fingers had attached them to the tree. The tree fairly glowed. "Now, that's what a proper Christmas tree should look like," said the Old Woman.

The Ugly Child sighed. "It's beautiful," he said, and his odd brown eyes twinkled deep in his crumply face. "Now, it must be time for the feast."

"Feast!" screamed the Old Woman. "Well, I never! A beggar shows up on my doorstep and invites — no, *orders* me — to prepare a feast! Let me tell you, you ugly brat — there hasn't been a scrap of food in this house for *weeks* — well, ah . . . days . . ."

The Ugly Child's face grew very still and sad. The Old Woman scrinkled her face and tried not to look at him but it seemed that grotesque brown countenance was everywhere; she could even see it with her eyes shut. "Actually," she muttered, "I believe there is an old ham bone . . . and maybe a potato or two. But no turnips! Not a single turnip!"

"What's a turnip?" asked the Ugly Child.

The soup kettle was humming on the hearth, bubbling to itself and turning the ham bone and some potatoes into a most excellent stew. The Old Woman threw in a pinch of this and a pinch of that and stirred it a couple of times. "Hmmm," she said, "it wouldn't be too bad if we just had some bread to go with it."

Next thing she knew she had a great big bowl and was measuring out flour and sugar and an egg and some milk. The Ugly Child stood by with his wrinkled brown face bent over the bowl. Now that she looked at him closely, the Old Woman could see that he did not really appear to be thin: actually he was stout and craggy, strong-looking, like a rock...strange, ugly little child.

When the bread was mixed, raised, kneaded, and raised again, the Old Woman patted it once for luck and tucked it into the oven. "There," she announced, "that takes care of the feast." She sat down with the comfortable sigh of a poor woman who was doing her best to accommodate an awkward guest. God would remember her generosity.

"What about the presents?" asked the Ugly Child suddenly. "There should be a present for each of us under the tree."

"Abominable child!" shrieked the Old Woman. "Here I am with an aching back and throbbing feet, having worked my fingers to the bone — the very bone! — to keep Christmas for you — not knowing at all whose brat you are — and now you must have a present too! I'll be bound — I don't know where a body could find a gift in *this* house — unless — no! — well . . ."

There *was* a buckle. Silver, it was, and very old. It was the only thing left to her of any value by her old mother, and she had planned to be buried with it on her dress. Nobody knew of the buckle except her. She thought longingly of how nice she would have looked, laid out in her coffin in her plain black dress, with the silver buckle glinting up like a last triumphant smile, astonishing the villagers by its unsuspected richness. But the Ugly Child's face — so heavy, so brown, so disappointed — "Oh!" she cried, "such a child! Such a day!" And she rattled off into the corner and there was a crackling of a bit of paper and a bustle of string and finally there it was — a package under the tree. The Old Woman was so preoccupied with her enterprise that she did not notice that the Ugly Child had rattled off into another corner and done some bustling of his own, and now there were two packages under the tree.

By now the sun had climbed, unnoticed, to the meridian, and was sliding downward on his blue toboggan sled toward the western rim of the world. As evening came on, the smell of the ham-bone stew and baking bread filled the hut. The Old Woman polished up her two pewter bowls and laid the table with a clean cloth and a pair of spoons. When everything was ready — the soup dished up, the bread sliced, she called the Ugly Child.

"Come and eat," she said as she lighted a candle and set it in the middle of the table. "Tut!" she cried then as the Ugly Child grabbed his spoon — "not till after I've asked the blessing: — For what we are about to receive, dear Lord, we thank Thee. *Now* —"

The spoons clinked and clanked against the bowls and the bread crunched as they bit into it. The candle sputtered and the fire sparkled and the feast, if that's what it was, was merry. The Old Woman told a few jokes and the Ugly Child laughed, and the sound of his laughter was so great it must have echoed clear up to the stars, for it filled the house to overflowing.

"Now, it's time for you to open your gift," said the Old Woman at last. "Of course, it's not much . . ." she handed him the little package — almost, no, not at all reluctantly.

The Ugly Child took the gift and turned it silently over and over in his hands. He seemed to be absorbing the whole weight and feel of it — the crackle of the paper, the silky feel of the string. At last he opened it.

And the smile that spread across his ugly face so transformed it that the last bit of resentment left the Old Woman forever. "A buckle!" he shouted. "A silver buckle! Of all things in the world, the one I most wanted!" And he threw his arms around the Old Woman and hugged and kissed her till she was quite worn out with all that love.

"Ah, now — it's nothing — nothing much —" she stammered, blushing to think of how she had hated to give it away. "Only a buckle —"

"Only a buckle! Why, it's the greatest, most beautiful, most valuable buckle in the whole world!" cried the Ugly Child. "And I'll wear it forever. You'll see —"

Suddenly he fell silent, and the Old Woman roused herself and looked around. Without her realizing it, dusk had fallen, and already the first stars were beginning to show in the sky. The Ugly Child rose and went to the window. "I must go," he said. "It's getting late."

"Already?" cried the Old Woman. "But wait — we've not had any music yet —"

The Ugly Child opened the door. Across the snow came the sound of the village church bells, clear as birds calling through the winter night. "There is the music," said the Ugly Child softly. "I must go. No — don't come out. I can find my way. Good night, Old Woman. And thank you — thank you —"

And he was gone.

The Old Woman sat on by the fire, rocking and grumping. She was aching tired but happy, in the strangest way. "Uproar," she said, nudging the old dog at her feet, "what a day its been, what a day its been. What a *Christmas* —"

Then she noticed the other gift, lying under the fir tree. Strange, she had forgotten to open her package. Now what had that Ugly Child found to leave her?

She squatted down and drew it out, surprised at its great weight. But it didn't rattle. Carefully she opened the string, and lifted back the paper. And as she did so, out came the sound of bells, and the sound of laughter, and the smell of ham-bone stew and baking bread, the light of a candle, the light of stars . . .

"I'll keep it forever," the Old Woman said.

Up in the sky, Star Mother had been watching for her Youngest Child to come home. She was fussing and fuming, like all good mothers, anxious to see her child home safe from his great adventure.

At last she saw him, trudging up the long slope of the great black night sky. She put on a shawl of moonlight and rushed out to meet him. "Well — how did it go?" she called. "Are you well? Was it a happy day?"

Youngest Child sighed, and leaned his spiky, yellow head against Star Mother's breast. "Oh, it was a *lovely* day," he told her sleepily. "And I'm . . . so . . . tired . . ."

"Wait," cried Star Mother. "Tell me about it. Tell me all about Christmas. Is that too much to ask?"

"It was — oh, Mother —" Youngest Child yawned and looked around at all his brothers and sisters with whom he would now take his place forever in the sky — "it was . . . enough," he said.